JAMES CAMERON'S AVATAR™

THE MOVIE SCRAPBOOK

WRITTEN BY

MARIA WILHELM AND

DIRK MATHISON

BASED ON THE MOTION PICTURE WRITTEN AND DIRECTED BY

JAMES CAMERON

HARPER FESTIVAL
An Imprint of HarperCollins Publishers

TRAINING
0700
-0800

HarperFestival is an imprint of HarperCollins Publishers.
James Cameron's Avatar: The Movie Scrapbook
© 2009 Twentieth Century Fox Film Corporation. JAMES CAMERON'S AVATAR is
a trademark of Twentieth Century Fox Film Corporation. All rights reserved.
Printed in the United States of America. No part of this book may be used or
reproduced in any manner whatsoever without written permission except in the
case of brief quotations embodied in critical articles and reviews. For information
address HarperCollins Children's Books, a division of HarperCollins Publishers,
10 East 53rd Street, New York, NY 10022.
www.harpercollinschildrens.com
Library of Congress catalog card number: 2009935249
ISBN 978-0-06-180124-2
Design by Joe Merkel
9 10 11 12 13   WOR   10 9 8 7 6 5 4 3 2 1
First Edition

DESTINATION: PANDORA

Explorers! You are about to leave on an amazing journey to a place very far from Earth. You will travel into the future on a huge spaceship, skidding past stars and planets and finally landing on a strange and magnificent moon called Pandora.

In many ways, Pandora is like Earth. Puffy white clouds flit across a bright blue sky. Forests are thick and green. There are valleys, plains, lakes, rivers, and lots of blue, blue ocean. And animals climb, crawl, roam, swim, and fly, just like those on Earth.

But Pandora is very different from Earth. The people who live there are ten feet tall, striped like tigers, and have blue skin. Most of the animals there have four eyes and six legs. There are mountains that float. And, oh yes, at night everything glows in rainbow colors.

There are some challenges on Pandora. You can't breathe the air without a special mask, and many of the things that live there are dangerous to humans.

Especially if you're not prepared.

Like all great explorers, planning for your expedition is very important. If you're going to scale a high mountain covered with ice and snow, you need warm clothing and climbing equipment. If you're exploring in the sea, you need scuba gear and a wet suit. And maybe a submarine.

When you go to Pandora, you'll need the right equipment. You'll need thick boots, light clothing for the heat, a large backpack, and bug spray. There are lots of nasty biting insects in the rain forest. Itchy!

This is your logbook. It tells you everything you could ever want to know about Pandora—and it will help guide you as you explore it. Exploring a strange place like Pandora may sound scary, but remember: You are already an explorer. You explore every day in the park, your school, even right where you live. Look around wherever you are now—you're exploring. So, are you ready to explore Pandora? Pack your imagination and let's go.

SECTION ONE: ARRIVING ON PANDORA

ISV VENTURE STAR

Pandora is very, very far away from Earth.

Scientists had to invent huge, powerful ships that could travel safely for such a long distance. They are called Interstellar Vehicles—or ISVs. To make the trip, these ships go so fast they could make it to the Earth's moon in less than two seconds.

One of the ships is called the ISV Venture Star.

The Venture Star is almost a mile long. It has engines that use something called *matter-antimatter fusion* in the same way cars use gasoline. Even though it travels incredibly fast, the Venture Star still takes more than five years to go from Earth to Pandora. But if you are a passenger on board, the trip will seem much shorter. That's because once you are on the ship, you will be sent into a special chamber where you will be put into a state called *cryosleep*. If you weren't sleeping, you'd be very bored. You'd also need a lot of food and water. Cryosleep helps save resources and makes the trip to Pandora seem much faster.

When the Venture Star gets close to Pandora, the crew prepares it for arrival. It takes months just to slow the ship down. When the ship starts to orbit Pandora, you will be awakened from cryosleep. It won't feel as if five years have passed. It will feel more like a very long night of sleep.

This will be your first chance to see Pandora and the planet it orbits, Polyphemus. You'll be amazed by what you see.

Your expedition to Pandora is about to begin.

VALKYRIE SHUTTLE

The ISV *Venture Star* is far too big to land on Pandora. There's a smaller craft, the *Valkyrie* shuttle, to take you from the *Venture Star* to the moon below.

The *Valkyrie* shuttle looks like the space shuttles of the early twenty-first century. But the *Valkyrie* is much bigger and faster.

The *Valkyrie* is also the only way to get supplies like medicine and special mining equipment to Pandora. And it is the only way people can get back to the *Venture Star* when it's time for them to return to Earth.

The shuttle's most important job is bringing unobtanium from Pandora to the *Venture Star* so that it can be shipped home.

Strap in tight before takeoff. It's a bumpy ride into Pandora's atmosphere. Just before the shuttle lands, it slows down and hovers briefly above the landing pad at Hell's Gate.

EXOPACK

An exopack is a light backpack that filters out things like carbon dioxide and hydrogen sulfide from the Pandoran air. Once the air is filtered, the clean air goes through tubes into a mask that you wear around your nose and mouth.

If a human left Hell's Gate without an exopack, he or she would die within a few minutes.

Imagine if a daisy were the size of a tree. Or a rabbit were as big as your bed. Or your best friend grew so tall her head scraped the ceiling. Everything is bigger on Pandora—the plants, the animals, and especially the Na'vi, the moon's ten-foot-tall residents. Like Earth, Pandora is filled with weird and wonderful things that will surprise you and sometimes scare you a little. Look up and you'll see a banshee screaming through the sky like a fighter jet. Or a fan lizard spinning like a Frisbee. Look down and you'll discover glowworms you can use as flashlights and dandetiger plants sparkling like magic wands.

Things look strange and different. But you've prepared for your expedition. You're an explorer, after all. You've strapped on your breathing mask. You've looked at your map. And you've studied your Na'vi-English phrase book. You know that when you meet a Na'vi child, or *'eveng*, you should say a *kaltxi* or "hello." You're ready to explore this amazing world.

HELL'S GATE

Hell's Gate (or Resources Development Administration Extra-Solar Colony 01) is your first stop. It's where the soldiers, miners, scientists, and all the other humans live. It's like a fort.

The name Hell's Gate is a joke. It's like hell—hot, dangerous, and dirty. And, as on all of Pandora, you can't breathe the air outside. Hell's Gate is surrounded by a high fence. Soldiers in guard towers scan for dangerous animals that could get over the fence. Other soldiers patrol the compound for smaller animals that could dig under it.

Outside the fence, there are machines that look like robot lawn mowers. They keep the jungle from growing over the base.

There's a meeting place and mess hall known as Hell's Kitchen—or, more correctly, the base commissary. Between the research labs and the shuttle landing zone, there's a basketball court. Be warned: If you want to shoot some hoops, you have to wear a mask to breathe.

UNOBTANIUM

When humans first studied Pandora, they discovered a strange, powerful rock they called *unobtanium*. This rock is able to make machines like computers, radios, and high-speed trains work more efficiently by helping electricity flow more easily. This is called *superconductivity*. Unobtanium has become very important to every country on Earth.

Because of its amazing properties, unobtanium is far more valuable than gold or diamonds.

Unobtanium cannot be found on Earth. That is why travel to Pandora has become so essential.

AVATARS

On some of the trips from Earth to Pandora, the ISV *Venture Star* carries a large tank that is used to grow the body of an avatar.

An avatar is a body that a human "driver" can use to see, hear, and touch the wonders of Pandora. The human can be miles away but still be able to see and feel the things that the avatar body is seeing and feeling.

In order to allow this communication, scientists invented something called a *psionic link unit*. This machine is like a radio that transmits the thoughts and personality of a human into the body of an avatar. When a human is linked to an avatar, she appears to be asleep—but she is fully awake inside the avatar. An avatar has no thoughts or feelings of its own. When a human is not being transmitted into it, the avatar goes to sleep.

On Pandora, avatars have been made that look like the native Na'vi.

Human drivers learn how to make an avatar move just like a real Na'vi. Avatars don't need an exopack to breathe.

The people who run the unobtanium mines had hoped that the avatars could be used to help humans befriend the Na'vi. But the real Na'vi don't trust the avatars; they think they're kind of creepy. Now avatars are used mostly by scientists to explore Pandora.

//// It looks like it would be easy to fall over in an AMP Suit, but it's actually very difficult. There are special machines called *gyroscopes* that keep the suit stable, even if a soldier is running down a hill or climbing over rocks. ////////

AMP SUIT

The AMP Suit is used on Pandora by soldiers who work in the rain forest.

AMP is short for Amplified Mobility Platform. Once a soldier is inside the suit, he becomes a thirteen-foot-tall giant. When his arm moves, the suit's arm moves. When he moves his legs, the AMP Suit walks. When he grabs something, the suit's hand reaches out and grabs it as well. The suit's robotic hands are so strong that they can crush a brick.

The suit has weapons built into it, including a cannon and a flamethrower. If a large animal like a mountain banshee or a hammerhead titanothere attacks, the soldier would be able to defend himself. Soldiers in an AMP Suit also don't have to worry about the millions of flying, stinging insects in the Pandoran rain forest. Even these insects can't bite through metal.

As you can imagine, the Na'vi are afraid of soldiers in AMP Suits, especially when they are cutting through their rain forests.

VEHICLES ON PANDORA

Like Earth, Pandora has a lot of different environments—forests, plains, rivers and streams, and regions with high mountains that, unlike those on Earth, float. You needed to take a giant spaceship, like the ISV *Venture Star*, to get to Pandora. Now that you're here, getting around requires different vehicles built for the rugged, dangerous terrain. There's something like a superjeep called a Swan that will get you over rough, uneven ground at high speeds. And various kinds of helicopters and shuttles carry troops and cargo and are outfitted with guns. A giant Excavator that churns the ground is needed for mining operations. So is a massive dump truck to cart away what the miners find. If you're doing research on islands and alongside rivers, you'll need a boat. There's one like a hovercraft with a motor as quiet as a whisper.

But you probably want to try out an AMP Suit and walk around like a giant robot.

DRAGON GUNSHIP

The Dragon Gunship is like a powerful flying tank. It has thick sides, or armor, and lots of guns, rockets, and missiles. It can carry thirty soldiers and their supplies. It's also outfitted with the latest spy gadgets. It can watch Pandora from the sky and protect soldiers on the ground.

AT-99 SCORPION GUNSHIP

The AT-99 Scorpion gunship is like a regular helicopter, but it is much faster and more powerful.

The Scorpion is bigger than a school bus and as fast as a racecar. It can fly straight up very fast.

The Scorpion was built for combat in cities and jungles on Earth. It has many powerful guns, including cannons, machine guns, and missiles.

The Na'vi hate the Scorpion, because it is incredibly loud. Sometimes, when it's flying overhead, its engines cause the sturmbeest to stampede.

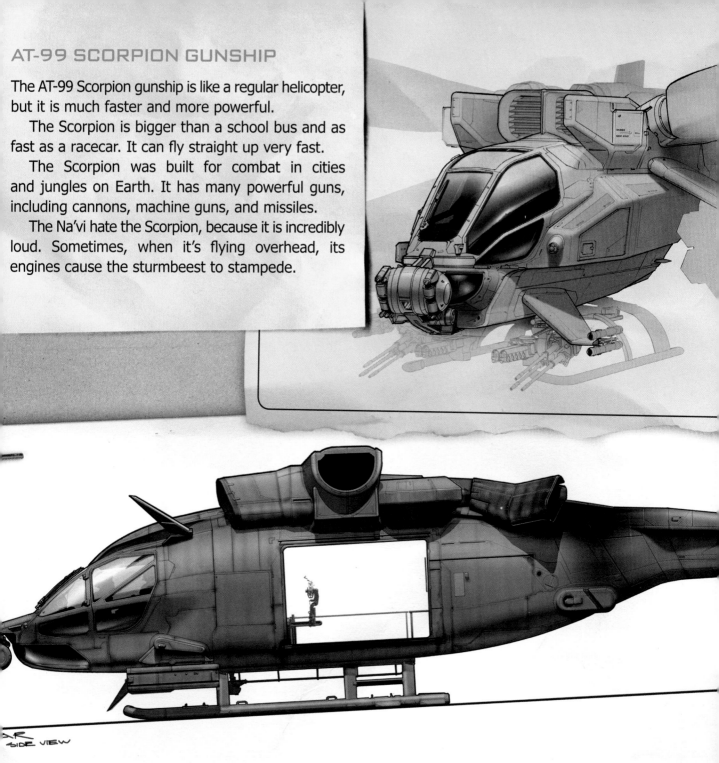

SIDE VIEW

SAMSON

The Samson Tiltrotor Utility Ship is a large helicopter. It can take off and land vertically. This means it can fly straight up in the air and land straight down in tight spaces.

The Samson zooms through the sky carrying scientists, avatars, and supplies to places far away from Hell's Gate, like the Hallelujah Mountains. It has a heavy-duty crane that takes large labs into Pandora's thick forests. Scientists do research there on plants and animals. If they're lucky, they sometimes meet up with Na'vi walking through the forest.

The Samson has computer-controlled rockets to defend itself against attack. The sides of the Samson are covered by thick steel plates, like a tank.

GAV SWAN

The GAV Swan is like a jeep. It is made to move soldiers from place to place over any landscape. It can't go fast, but it has the power to climb over hills and boulders. The Swan is also used to gather intelligence or to take workers on Pandora into areas where there are no roads.

The Swan has six tires that are made from strong materials such as titanium to help them over rough terrain.

It's nicknamed the Swan because it has a special chair that can be raised high above the vehicle. When the chair is up, it looks like a swan's long neck reaching out. Soldiers in the chair are particularly vulnerable. All they have to protect them is the armor they're wearing. But from that high up, the soldiers can get a better view of what's nearby.

SLASH-CUTTER

Pandora's thick forests and towering trees make it hard to mine for unobtanium. The fastest way is to turn a forest into wood chips and sawdust by using a Slash-Cutter.

The Slash-Cutter can slice through trees as wide and tall as an ancient redwood in under a minute. A ripper machine works with the Slash-Cutter. It hooks onto tree stumps and any other parts of the forest that are left standing.

The Na'vi hate the Slash-Cutter and what it has done to Pandora's forests.

EXCAVATOR

One of the biggest and most powerful machines on Pandora is the Excavator. It looks like a big truck, but it has special attachments to strip away dirt and rock so that miners can get to the unobtanium beneath the ground.

The Excavator is the size of a big ship and has huge, powerful engines.

Inside the cab, the operators get information about what's going on with the Excavator from a display board attached to their helmets. This allows them to keep their attention focused on the action outside.

Like many of the machines, the Excavator is very loud and destructive. But it is very helpful to the unobtanium miners, who could not do their work without it.

RDA BOAT

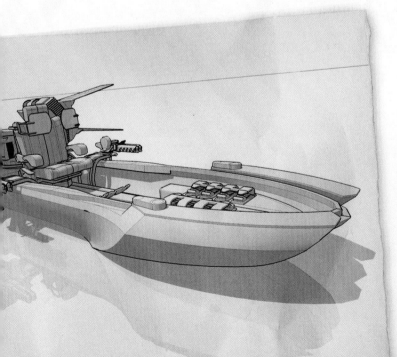

The Na'vi call the RDA boat a "canoe that skims." The boat is built with technology that lets it hover just above the water. It's very useful for traveling over Pandora's swamps, where the water isn't very deep.

The boat is more than nine feet long and more than three feet wide. It takes two pilots to drive it. It has a special engine that can go into something called *hush mode*, which allows the boat to travel without making noise.

The RDA boat has guns on the front and is used to protect bigger boats from attack. It also transports small teams of avatars to islands and riverbanks, where they do scientific research.

SECTION THREE: HOMETREE

Imagine a tree house as huge as the Great Pyramid in Egypt. That is how big Hometree is. Like the Great Pyramid, Hometree has lots of hidden caves and secret alcoves within it.

Hometree is where the Na'vi of the *Omaticaya*, or Blue Flute Clan, live. Nestled deep in the forest, Hometree twists up in a pattern that looks like a bee's honeycomb.

The Na'vi leave Hometree every day to hunt for food. At night, they head back to Hometree to sleep and eat with their families, to talk about the day, to tell jokes, and to share the history of their ancestors. There's a lot of storytelling, singing, and dancing at Hometree. It is a very happy place.

Hometree glows with the warm, golden light of lanterns filled with firefly-like insects. Mountain banshees, brightly colored flying creatures with leathery wings, nest in its highest branches to be closer to their Na'vi riders.

Hometree is the center of the Na'vi's way of life. It is their home.

THE NA'VI

In many ways, the Na'vi are like humans. They speak to one another. They cook, tell stories, sing, dance, and play instruments. They are hunters, warriors, and great artists. They value many of the same things we do. And they are very spiritual creatures who are devoted to a godlike being called Eywa.

The name *Na'vi* means "people." Na'vi are normally peaceful, but they become fierce when threatened.

Na'vi have human features, but they look quite different from us. They have stripes like tigers. They have four toes on each foot and three fingers and one thumb on each hand. And they have a tail to help them balance as they jump from tree limb to limb.

Na'vi men average about ten feet tall. Women are slightly shorter. The Na'vi are much stronger and faster than we are. They also have shimmering marks on their body that glow. This is called *bioluminescence*, and it helps Na'vi identify one another.

There are many different Na'vi groups called *clans* all over Pandora. The *Omaticaya* are the Na'vi at Hometree. They are the closest to the humans at Hell's Gate. Most of what we know about these intelligent creatures comes from learning about the *Omaticaya*.

THE NA'VI QUEUE

The Na'vi have an antenna, sort of like a bee's. A long, thick braid called a *queue* covers the antenna. It may be the most special part of a Na'vi.

A queue is sort of like a plug. It connects the Na'vi to one another and to certain animals and trees much like a plug connects a lamp to electricity. It provides the Na'vi with information about his world.

Using their queue, every Na'vi warrior connects with a mountain banshee. This connection will last forever. Na'vi can also connect with a direhorse. Even these animals become calm and friendly when Na'vi connect to them.

Na'vi Queue

NA'VI CHILDREN

Na'vi children love to learn. Their days are very busy. They study how to hunt, ride, fly, and use tools. They're taught to play musical instruments and to sing special songs about things that are important to them. Na'vi children also learn to honor their world in art and dance, and to tell stories. Storytelling is very important to the Na'vi. Stories are a way to remember the history of their families and to teach important lessons about how to care for Pandora and for one another.

All the things the Na'vi do make up their culture. The Na'vi love Pandora, and their rich and wonderful culture celebrates the beautiful moon they live on.

FIRE PIT

The Na'vi of Hometree (the *Omaticaya*) cook most of their food together around a large fire pit.

Na'vi children grow up near the warmth of the fire. It is a great place to hear stories, learn songs, and tell jokes. The Na'vi call the fire pit *mreki u'lito.* It is usually a long trench that is surrounded by rocks.

The Na'vi of Hometree say that the fire in the fire pit has not gone out in more than a hundred years. It is very important to have a fire ready for any hunter who brings back an animal that he has killed. The Na'vi believe it is vital to honor the animal that gave up its life for the good of the clan. They think that a fire that has gone out would be disrespectful to both the hunter and the animal that died.

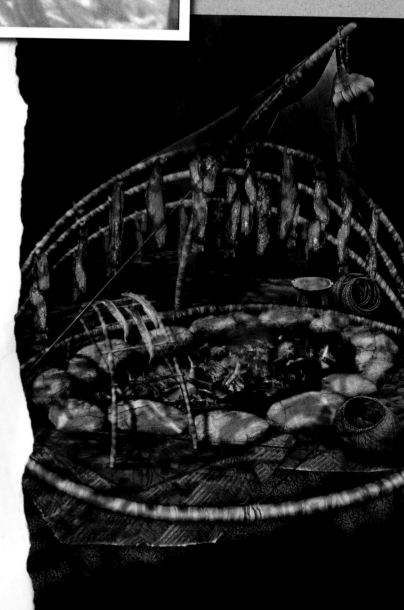

LOOM

The Na'vi don't make things like cars or computers. But they are amazing craftsmen.

The Na'vi of Hometree are famous for making fabrics and clothes. They have looms of different sizes. The loom occupies a place of honor in the common area of Hometree. The Na'vi call this the Mother Loom. It is made of ropes and wood attached to the branches of Hometree. It is here that the Na'vi make hammocks, ropes, and mats as well as clothes and other decorations.

The Na'vi have different words for loom. The most common literally means "many branches together are strong." The loom also makes the Na'vi think of Eywa, who is the great spirit of Pandora. When they are making a certain kind of fabric, they call the loom "Eywa's wisdom is revealed to all of us." That the Na'vi use Eywa and Hometree to describe the loom shows how important the loom is to them.

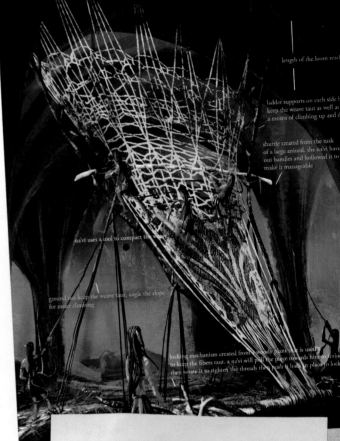

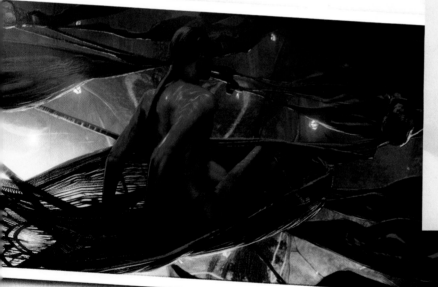

LOOM SONGS

Like the firepit, the loom is a place where the Na'vi tell stories and sing songs. Here are a few lyrics from one of the songs they like to sing:

Katot täftxu oel (I weave the rhythm)
Nìean nìrim (In yellow and blue),
Ayzìsìtä kato (The rhythm of the years),
'Ìheyu sìreyä (The spiral of the lives),
'Ìheyu sìreyä (The spiral of the lives),
Sìreyä le-Na'vi (Lives of the People)
Oeru teya si (Fills me),
Oeru teya si (Fills me).

HAMMOCKS

The Na'vi sleep on hammocks in large groups, protected by the branches and leaves of Hometree. They build beautiful, big hammocks of all different sizes. There are hammocks for one person. There are hammocks for couples. There are even hammocks big enough for whole families.

There are several different names for hammocks. One Na'vi phrase for hammocks means "Eywa cradles everyone." Another name just means "us."

The hammocks are made from many different materials, including twine made from vines, fibrous leaves, and beanstalk palm fronds. They are usually decorated with different patterns, shells, and feathers. Na'vi hammocks can last for more than twenty years.

Family elders decide when a new hammock is needed. It takes a few months to make a hammock, and everyone helps. Na'vi families are happy to work on it together—making a hammock is a time for celebration.

HOMETREE SONGS

Listen and you'll hear the Na'vi singing. While they sleep, the Na'vi dream the songs they sing. Songs also come to them when they wander in the forest alone. When their queues are connected to an animal, new songs sometimes dance in their minds.

Na'vi songs are colorful musical stories about playing games, cooking, taking care of children, and weaving. There are also songs about great battles and great hunts. Many songs for children teach important things like hunting, riding animals, or making fires for cooking. How would you know which animals are friendly and which are not? Or what's good to eat or will make you sick? Na'vi songs help you understand the world of Pandora.

When Na'vi children are with their parents, they sometimes sing together quietly. They sing about the history of the Na'vi people and their connection to all living things.

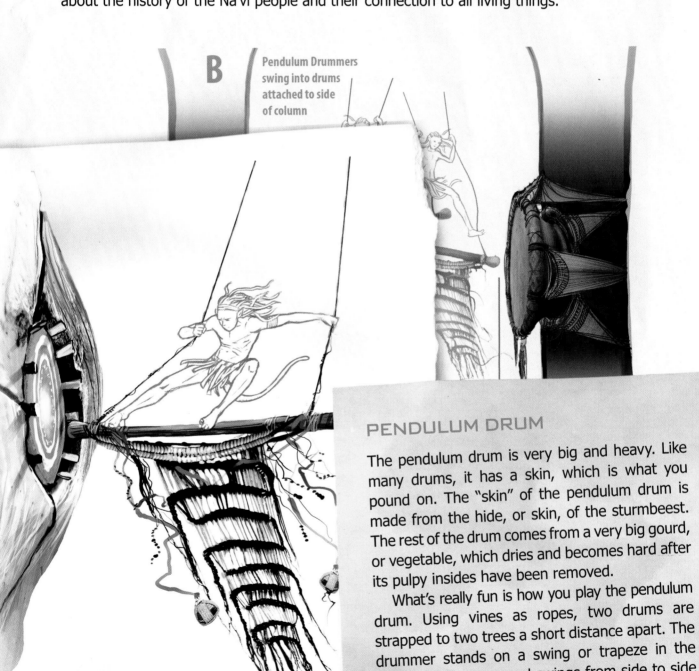

B Pendulum Drummers swing into drums attached to side of column

PENDULUM DRUM

The pendulum drum is very big and heavy. Like many drums, it has a skin, which is what you pound on. The "skin" of the pendulum drum is made from the hide, or skin, of the sturmbeest. The rest of the drum comes from a very big gourd, or vegetable, which dries and becomes hard after its pulpy insides have been removed.

What's really fun is how you play the pendulum drum. Using vines as ropes, two drums are strapped to two trees a short distance apart. The drummer stands on a swing or trapeze in the middle of the trees and swings from side to side between two drums, hitting each of them and making lots of noise.

THE BLUE FLUTE

The Na'vi who live at Hometree call themselves the Blue Flute Clan.

There is an actual blue flute that is hidden deep within the branches of Hometree. No human has ever seen the flute. It is taken out only on rare, special occasions. Only the male clan leader is allowed to play it. The flute has only one hole, like a penny whistle. When it is played, it makes only one or two notes.

The Na'vi believe that Eywa made the flute by plucking a branch from Hometree. Eywa gave it to the Na'vi so that they could communicate with her and with their ancestors.

That's why the blue flute is so special to the Na'vi.

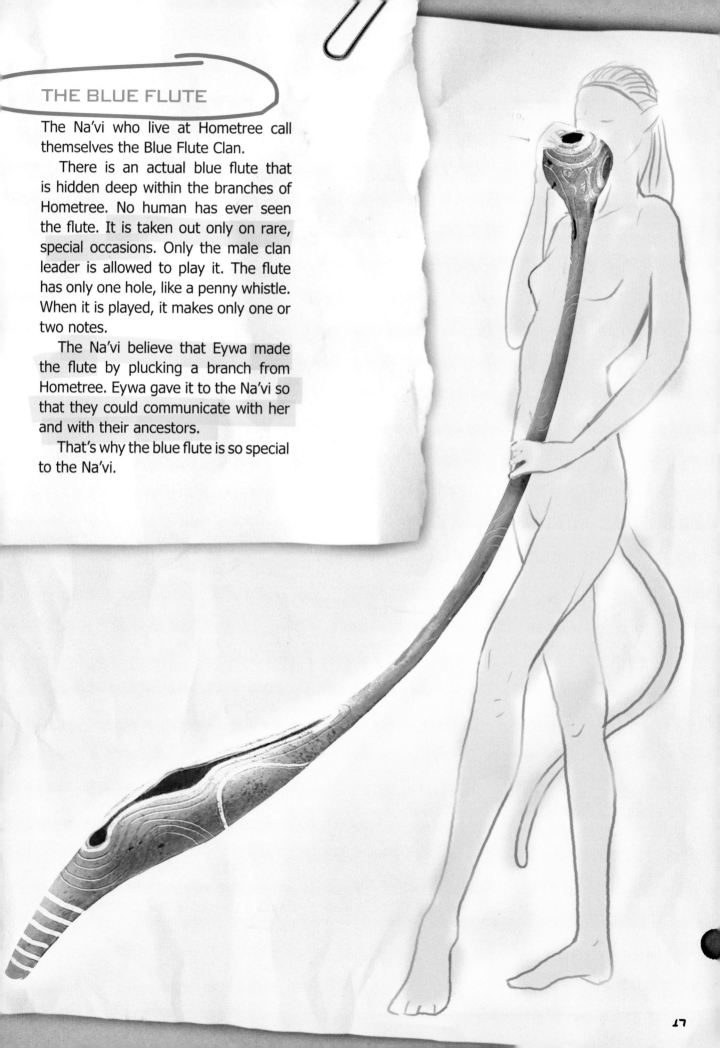

TEYLU

A teylu looks like a fat worm. It's really a grub, which is a type of insect larva, or baby insect. The Na'vi love teylu. Along with steaming them like shrimp, they roast them over a fire with vegetables and serve them on a stick, like a shish kebab.

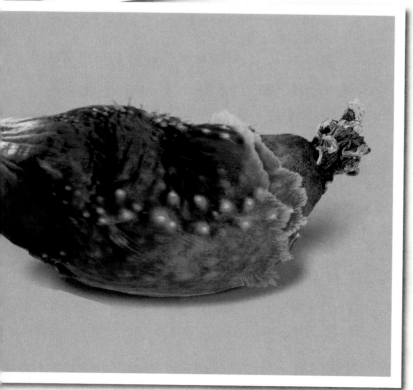

PUSH FRUIT

There is a fruit that the Na'vi call *uta mauti*, or "push fruit." It grows high in the rain forest in a push fruit tree.

Because it's hard to pick, it's considered a special treat. If Na'vi happen to find one on the ground, it is considered such good luck that they will take the fruit home to show their friends what they've found.

It is considered good manners for the finder to offer the fruit to a friend. It's also considered good manners to refuse to take the fruit. But Na'vi kids like to pretend to take a bite before giving it back. Everyone laughs at this, because it would be extremely rude to accept a lucky push fruit from the person who found it in the forest.

STINGBAT

The Na'vi do not have pets like cats or dogs. The closest they get is a stingbat, which they call *riti*.

Stingbats are like huge, mean vampire bats.

They have big fangs and sharp claws. The stingbat gets its name from the stinger on the end of its tail. The stinger can deliver venom that is very dangerous to humans.

Some Na'vi treat the animals like trained parakeets. They are able to call to a stingbat with a clicking sound that they make. The stingbat will fly down and land on a Na'vi's arm or shoulder and then eat fruit from the Na'vi's hand.

The stingbat is an omnivore. This means that it eats fruits and vegetables as well as meat. The stingbat lives in the treetops in the rain forest (the canopy), where it can catch rodents and eat fruit.

Stingbats have very small brains and are really not the brightest animals on Pandora. They are easy prey for bigger animals, such as the banshee.

DAKTERON

The Na'vi call the dakteron an insect eater because it does just that—eats pesky insects.

The dakteron plant is great at climbing trees. It traps insects by luring them with an odor that smells as good to them as chocolate-chip cookies right out of the oven do to you. Insects land on the leaves looking for food and, surprise, they're gobbled up by the plant.

The Na'vi are smart. They plant the sneaky dakteron in places where biting insects bother them. The dakteron tempts the insects with the way it smells, and then it eats them for lunch.

Hometree is in one of Pandora's vast and beautiful rain forests. The Na'vi word for the rain forest is *na'ring*. It is their home and the source of everything they need to survive and be happy.

At twilight, the rain forest shimmers with light from billions of different plants and animals.

In the rain forest, the Na'vi find plants that can be used for food or to make things like medicine, baskets, tents, and hammocks. They also hunt animals for food and clothing here. The Na'vi use bows, arrows, axes, and knives on their hunts. Their weapons are very practical but also very beautiful. They are decorated to help the Na'vi honor the animals of the rain forest, one another, and even Eywa.

Pandora's rain forest is a place of mystery and danger. There are huge, fierce animals with sharp claws and venomous stingers. Some of these animals can swoop out of the sky or rumble through the tall trees. There are also nasty stinging bugs and vicious biting fish. Even the Na'vi are afraid of some things in the rain forest.

But this is the Na'vi's home. It is here that they feel most connected to nature and to one another.

Some areas of the rain forest are considered sacred. This means that they are places that the Na'vi go to feel connected to Eywa.

On your journey to Pandora, you will be amazed at the sights and sounds of the rain forest. But despite the beauty of your surroundings, you must be very careful.

VIPERWOLF

A lot of things on Pandora look scary until you get to know them better and see just how amazing and beautiful they really are.

Discovering wonderful things on Pandora sometimes takes time. You have to see what's familiar or strange in a new way. What seems ugly at first may really be beauty in disguise.

Few animals embody this idea more than the viperwolf. They look scary. But they are fiercely intelligent animals. They hunt in packs, like wolves and coyotes do. With bright green eyes, they can see perfectly in both daylight and at night. And their blue stripes, or "banding," actually glow in the dark.

The viperwolf's head is shaped like a snake's—with rows of very sharp, transparent fangs that look like dirty icicles. Viperwolves also hiss when they're mad, just like snakes do.

Viperwolves live in the rain forest and in other places on Pandora. They have few enemies. Like chimps, gorillas, and people, they have opposable thumbs. They can hold and grab things like humans can. They can also climb trees and cling to tree limbs while looking for food.

Viperwolves can talk, but not in a language you can understand. Like coyotes in the night, they yip and yelp.

HEXAPEDE

Hexapedes are one of the most beautiful and fragile creatures on Pandora. The Na'vi call them *yerik*. Hexapedes have a long beard and six legs. They live in the plains, the rain forests, and the mountains of Pandora. They are herbivores, meaning they eat only plants, fruits, nuts, and seeds.

The hexapede is important to the Na'vi. It is the first animal a young Na'vi is allowed to hunt. It is also the main source of food and clothing for the Na'vi. Hexapede leather is also used to make weapons as well as musical instruments.

Because the Na'vi consider these creatures to be so important, they put pictures of the hexapede on clothes and on shields. Hexapedes are gentle creatures, which makes them easy prey for many of Pandora's other animals. They can run fast and can turn very quickly. They also have two horns with a piece of skin between them. When a hexapede stretches its horn skin, the hexapede looks bigger and scarier to other animals. They can smell other animals from far away, which helps them avoid danger.

SLINGER

A slinger is two bodies in one. There's a "mother" body and a "baby" body. The mother body is everything from the neck down and the baby body is the head, which is shaped like a triangle and has fangs. The slinger lives in the rain forest and dines on hexapedes.

The slinger may seem lazy and goofy, but it is not harmless. When it spots a hexapede, for example, it slings its head like a dart. Once the fangs puncture the skin, the head releases its poisons into the wounded animal and then squeals for the mother body to come join it. The headless "mother" finds the "baby" through the sounds it makes. When she does, she extends her neck and reattaches with the head. And then they have dinner.

But just as babies grow up, so does the head of the slinger, which will get too big for the mother body over time. When it does, it leaves the mother and grows its own full body with its own dart-head. Left behind and unable to feed itself, the headless mother body soon dies.

PROLEMURIS

These chattering little creatures live high in the trees of the rain forest. This keeps them safe from dangerous animals on the ground, but not safe from dangerous animals in the sky.

If a prolemuris spots you, he'll run away, making a chirpy, high-pitched squeal. Like many animals, he's more scared of you than you are of him.

Prolemuris can grow to be about as tall as a table. Their ears will often point in different directions. It looks funny. But it helps the prolemuris hear animals nearby and stay safe.

Prolemuris have strong teeth, which are as sharp as needles. This helps them chew tough Pandoran vegetation. They eat just plants, fruits, and insects.

Prolemuris can "fly" (actually, they glide by falling slowly) using the special flaps of skin that grow under their arms. Leaping from a branch, they can go the length of about five cars. Their bones are hollow, which makes them very light and able to travel far.

Even when they're not moving from tree to tree, prolemuris jump across tree branches faster than most humans run on flat ground. Prolemuris also have great eyesight and coordination.

FAN LIZARD

The fan lizard is about as long as a computer keyboard. It comes out mostly at night to lick the sweet sap off trees and nibble insects. It lolls around in Pandora's swamps and hides in giant ferns during the day.

Young Na'vi love to taunt and tease fan lizards by running through fields where the lizards are resting. When frightened, the lizards transform into something like fans and fly away to the safety of the nearest branch.

THANATOR

The thanator is one of the biggest, fiercest animals on Pandora.

There is really nothing like it on Earth. Instead of fur, the thanator has skin that looks like black metal. Its skin is very tough, and it helps protect the thanator from attack. The thanator can grow to be the size of a minivan. Its teeth are nine inches long and its jaws can open very wide.

Like most land animals on Pandora, the thanator has six legs. Its wide tail can be used like a club to hurt animals it wants to eat, or to defend itself. It can sense another animal from miles away with something on its head called sensory quills.

The thanator is also very strong, fast, and smart.

The thanator likes to hunt alone at night. It prefers to eat meat, but it also eats leaves and fruit. The thanator fears only other thanators and the great leonopteryx.

DINICTHOID

In the lakes of Pandora you'll find dinicthoid, a fierce, fast, and furious fish.

Dinicthoids have a big appetite. Their teeth are like razors. They eat anything and everything—big fish, small fish, plants, and even seeds.

Dinicthoids are fierce pretenders. They use light to make their bodies look bigger or smaller to attract the unsuspecting seafood dinner. Na'vi like to eat the dinicthoids if they can catch one. That's hard to do!

If you want a dinicthoid for a pet, you'd have to get a large aquarium with very thick glass. Dinicthoids get angry when they're confined, and they'll slam into the walls of the tank. Yes, they're fierce, fast, and sometimes furious fish.

FISHING ARROW

The Na'vi use a special arrow to catch fish. The Na'vi fishing arrow has a head that is made from a seedpod that looks like a three-pronged steak knife. The shape of the seedpod is perfect for fishing because it helps the arrow stay inside the fish. The Na'vi put feathers on the end of the arrowhead to make it fly straighter. It takes a lot of skill and practice to catch fish the Na'vi way.

The arrow is connected to a string so that fish cannot swim away. The string allows the Na'vi to reel in a fish after it's been caught.

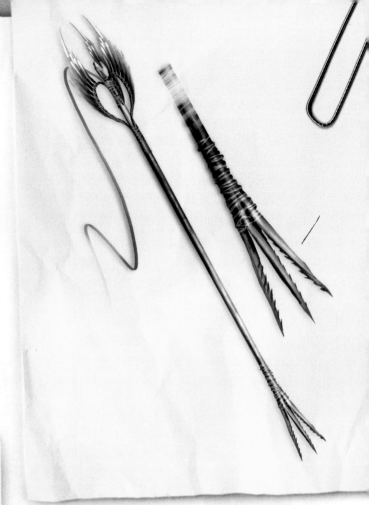

BOUND-ON HOOKS THAT CATCH ON THE ROPE

WEAPON: BOLA

BOLAS

The Na'vi have many different weapons for hunting. Sometimes, they want to catch an animal without hurting it. For example, a Na'vi hunter would much rather trap a viperwolf than injure it, even if the viperwolf is threatening.

To trap an animal without hurting it, a Na'vi hunter would probably use a bola. A bola is a rope that is about four feet long. It is weighted at the ends with heavy, polished seeds. A skilled Na'vi hunter can throw the bola and make it wrap around the legs of an animal. The animal trips and is trapped by the rope.

It takes many years to get good at throwing a bola. Na'vi children start practicing with the bola when they are very young. First they practice on tree limbs. When they are older, they are allowed to try to catch a hexapede.

By the time they are grown, most Na'vi hunters can catch an animal using a bola. The bola may not seem very powerful. But a skilled hunter can make even a galloping sturmbeest fall down.

NA'VI STREAMERS

Streamers are like flags that tell you which clan a Na'vi comes from. They are made from animal skins that are put on frames or poles made of wood. Sometimes Na'vi put streamers on their direhorses as decorations.

The Na'vi put drawings of things that are important to them on their streamers. The *U'imi huyuticaya*, a Na'vi clan, have great respect for the viperwolf, so they put a picture of it on their streamers.

PLANTS OF PANDORA

The trees, plants, and flowers on Pandora are amazing. Most of the plants are bigger than plants on Earth because there is less gravity pulling them down. The trees grow to twice the size of the tallest tree on Earth. Many plants survive by eating insects or small animals. Some of the plants can slap you as you walk by. There are others that help clean the air and the soil. At night, most plants glow in rainbow colors. It's like being at an amusement park.

The most amazing of all are the life forms that are half plant and half animal. They are called *zooplantae* or, as a kind of joke, *planimals*. They have the ability to feel and react to things in a way that is more "intelligent" than plants on Earth. But if you saw them you'd think they were plants.

There are people on Pandora called xenobotanists who are studying all these remarkable plants to see what new information they can bring back to use on Earth.

BIOLUMINESCENCE

Most of the plants and animals on Pandora have marks that glow. This is called *bioluminescence*. Bioluminescence happens when certain chemicals in the plant or animal mix together. This chemical reaction gives off light, but not heat. If you were to touch a glowing plant on Pandora, it would feel cool.

Bioluminescence is everywhere on Pandora. For instance, the Pandoran anemonoid is a common Pandoran water creature. Anemonoids glow in all sorts of beautiful colors because of bioluminescence.

Bioluminescence comes in every color there is, but bioluminescent plants usually glow blue or green.

There is even bioluminescent moss on Pandora. When you step on this moss, ripples of light go out from your foot, like when you throw a pebble into a pond.

Some scientists think that bioluminescence is a way for creatures to be able to spot others of their kind. Some animals can turn off their bioluminescence so that other animals can't see them coming. Other animals can use glowing marks to make them seem bigger and scarier than they really are.

The Na'vi have markings, too. Their markings help the Na'vi identify one another, even in the dark.

when it's shrunk

BAJA TICKLER

The baja tickler is a strange and special plant that cleans the air on Pandora. That makes it very important to the planet and to the Na'vi. It's also very dangerous. Built like a hollow tree, the baja tickler sucks in poisons and turns them into a liquid that it stores inside itself. When the plant gets too full of the liquid poisons, it sprays a poison liquid out its top. The Na'vi are very careful around this plant because it's hard to know when it'll spray.

HELICORADIAN

Have you ever seen a Venus flytrap? When an insect lands on tiny hairs on this plant, the flytrap snaps shut to capture and eat it. This is called a "sensitive" plant because it moves when something touches it.

The helicoradian is also a sensitive plant. When something touches it, it curls up. And then, in the blink of an eye, special roots suck the plant down into the ground. Other helicoradian plants simply sense when danger is near and sink into the ground even without being touched.

The helicoradian is like a cross between a plant and an animal. It has a nervous system, which is something that animals have. Scientists are still trying to figure out how this works.

The Na'vi have learned to use the helicoradian to alert them to danger. If they see or hear a helicoradian curling up, they know that a large animal is probably nearby. The Na'vi also use its leaves as robes for special ceremonies and to make paints.

10-11 ft tall

BINARY SUNSHINE

The binary sunshine plant has leaves that glow brightly enough to be used as lights. But they are more useful than an ordinary lamp. Their leaves turn different colors when the land around them is safe and when there's danger.

The Na'vi use the glowing leaves of the binary sunshine plant to show them where it is safe to cross in the forest. That's why this plant is also called a "danger teller," or as it's known in the Na'vi language, *penghhrap*.

BINARY SUNSHINE

CHALICE PLANT

There are many plants on Pandora that are carnivores. This means that they survive by eating insects or small animals.

The largest carnivorous plant ever found is the chalice plant. It lives in the rain forests of Pandora and can grow as tall as a house. The Na'vi call it *yomioang*, which means "animal eater."

The chalice plant makes a sweet-smelling nectar that attracts animals to it. When a small animal crawls inside the plant to get the nectar, it gets trapped and eaten by the plant.

Even the Na'vi fear the plant, which can grow big enough to swallow a full-grown man. Na'vi children learn about the dangers of the plant when they are very little and are taught a funny song and dance that helps them remember to stay away from the plant.

OCTOSHROOM

Lots of things grow very large on Pandora, and the octoshroom does, too. It is like a mushroom that's as big as a baby elephant.

The octoshroom feeds on what's in Pandora's soil and takes poisons out of the dirt. A tea made from its roots protects against the venom of spiders, scorpions, and other insects whose bite can make you sick.

POPSICLE PLANT

The popsicle plant looks like something you would find at an amusement park or a candy store. It is chubby and has bright stripes. That's why humans call it a popsicle plant.

But the Na'vi know better. They call it *somtilor*, which means "hot beauty."

The popsicle plant is very important to the health of Pandora. The plant absorbs dangerous, radioactive things in the soil and air and then stores them inside it.

Because of these radioactive elements, popsicle plants can become very warm. The Na'vi know that it's best to stay away from them.

Scientists wonder if the popsicle plant could be used on Earth, too. It's possible that this plant could help clean up areas that are polluted.

POPSICLE PLANT

TWISTED LILY

Imagine you're walking by a tall plant and suddenly, the plant reaches out and slaps you with one of its leaves.

That's what would happen if you were on your journey on Pandora and you walked too close to a twisted lily.

The twisted lily is a planimal, and though it may seem vicious, it doesn't want to hurt you. It just wants you to stay away. When an animal gets close to it, the plant senses this and its bioluminescent markings start to glow. This sends a message to the rest of the plant that an animal is nearby. Then, the plant's stems twist and turn in the direction of the animal. They are able to give the animal a slap hard enough to discourage it from eating the plant.

The Na'vi call this plant *minyu*, which means "turner."

Na'vi kids love to play with this plant. They run up to it to see if they can get away from the flapping leaves. One of their favorite games is to push their friends into the *minyu* and watch them get whacked.

WOODSPRITE

Woodsprites are the seeds of a willow-like tree found only on Pandora. Woodsprites are part plant, part animal, and all angel.

The woodsprite's trees are very different from any willow you'd find on Earth. They are found in forests and mountains, and they are very important to the Na'vi. The Na'vi call these glowing, fluffy woodsprites *atokirina*. Woodsprites float on a breeze and are important messengers. They tell the Na'vi about their future or help them see something important that's going on in their world now. Even the Na'vi sometimes need help understanding the significance of what they see.

UNIDELTA TREE

The unidelta tree is a tall, straight tree that is very useful to the Na'vi. Wood from the unidelta tree is very strong. The Na'vi carve canoes from it and also use it to make canoe paddles, spears, and other tools for hunting.

The tree can grow to be thirty feet high. This would be a big tree on Earth. But on Pandora, where some of the trees can grow to more than four hundred feet, the unidelta is not considered very tall.

The leaves from the unidelta tree are covered in a kind of wax. The Na'vi melt the wax to use to make baskets waterproof. Since the leaves themselves are waterproof, the Na'vi fold them to use as bowls.

The roots of the tree contain a poison, so animals and the Na'vi stay away from them.

LEAF DETAIL

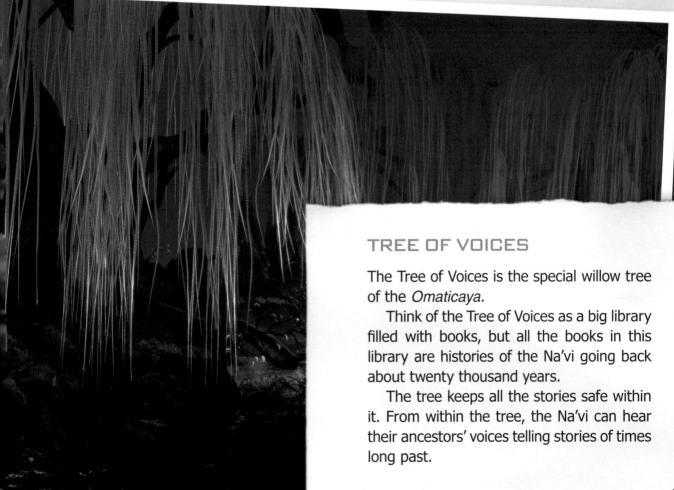

TREE OF VOICES

The Tree of Voices is the special willow tree of the *Omaticaya*.

Think of the Tree of Voices as a big library filled with books, but all the books in this library are histories of the Na'vi going back about twenty thousand years.

The tree keeps all the stories safe within it. From within the tree, the Na'vi can hear their ancestors' voices telling stories of times long past.

Pandora isn't all dense forests and jungles. There are wide-open spaces that are green with grass and aren't packed with trees and plants. These are called the plains. On the Pandoran plains you'll find areas with river deltas that have many streams, ponds, and rumbling rivers.

You will see animals here that you probably would not see deep in the rain forest.

DIREHORSE

By their nature, direhorses are calm, peaceful, and intelligent creatures.

The Na'vi love and respect the direhorse, and sing songs and tell stories about them.

Direhorses are somewhat like Earth horses, but much bigger. They have six legs and four eyes. They can run as fast as a car.

Direhorses also have two long, thin antennae on their heads. Direhorses like to touch their antennae to the antennae of other direhorses. Scientists think they do this to be affectionate, similar to when humans hold hands. But they also do it to find out if there are any dangerous animals or food nearby.

When a Na'vi hunter wants to bond with a direhorse, the hunter will jump onto its back. Then the hunter will take his queue and touch it to one of the direhorse's antennae. When the queue and the antenna link together, a bond is formed.

Once the Na'vi and a direhorse are linked, they become like one creature. The link allows a Na'vi to communicate mentally with the animal. The hunter need only think, Turn right, and the direhorse will turn right.

DIREHORSE BOW

When the Na'vi are riding on the back of a direhorse, she uses a direhorse bow.

The direhorse bow is designed to be easy to use while riding. The bow is almost as tall as a Na'vi. Its string is made from the stomach of a sturmbeest, and its handle is hexapede leather.

When hunters are old enough, they are allowed to carve their first bow from wood that comes from Hometree. This is an important moment in the life of young hunters. It means that they are ready for the challenges of being an adult.

DIREHORSE PITCHER PLANT

The direhorse pitcher plant produces a sweet nectar that the direhorse loves to drink.

The plant is shaped like a water pitcher, and when the direhorse puts its long nose into it, its nose gets covered with a sticky part of a flower hidden inside. The sticky part is called pollen.

The direhorse takes pitcher plant pollen from plant to plant just like bees on Earth do. This helps the plants reproduce.

STURMBEEST

Sturmbeest lumber along like trucks on a crowded highway. Sturmbeest hang out in big groups called herds. They spend most of the day near the banks of Pandora's rivers. Using the horny part of their jaws, they dig in the soft, wet dirt for grubs and other insects.

Sturmbeest can't see well, but they can smell and hear threats from miles away. When they're afraid, they herd together to protect one another. If that doesn't work, they stampede, where the whole herd runs together in the same direction. When they stampede, it sounds like a jet taking off.

The Na'vi hunt the sturmbeest. No other animal on Pandora provides the Na'vi with as many resources. The Na'vi use the sturmbeest for food, clothing, and decorations. The sturmbeest is so essential to the Na'vi way of life that the Na'vi sing sturmbeest songs and do sturmbeest dances to celebrate the animal.

HUNT SONGS

The Na'vi love to gather into groups and sing songs. But it is not just for fun. The Na'vi sing songs to pay respect to each other, to learn lessons, and to honor the living things on Pandora.

Many of their songs are about hunting. Songs about hunting are usually sung in a big group and are very rhythmical and energetic. Someone usually plays drums during the singing.

Some of the songs are sung before a big hunt. These songs ask for the hunters to be worthy of the task ahead. Other songs are performed as celebration after a good hunt. These songs are usually about how brave and strong the hunter and animals were during the hunt. Sometimes, the hunters even sing during the hunt. This helps give them courage and keeps them focused on what they are doing.

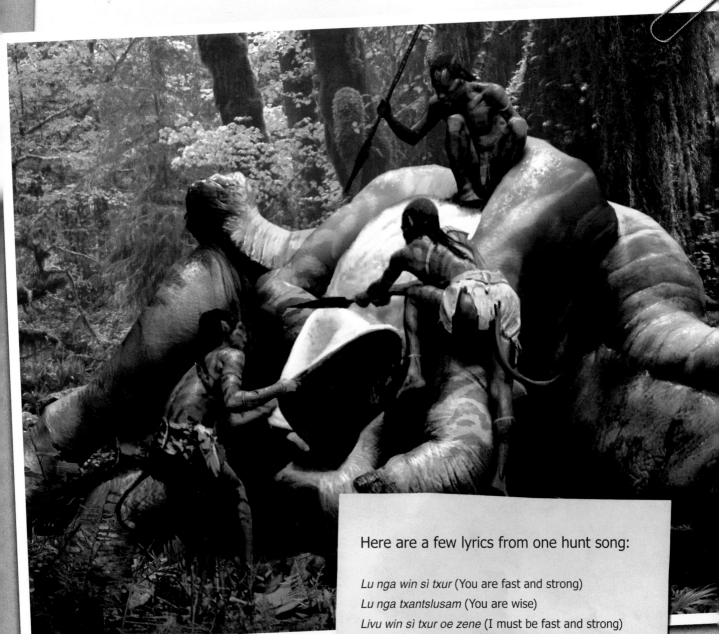

Here are a few lyrics from one hunt song:

Lu nga win sì txur (You are fast and strong)
Lu nga txantslusam (You are wise)
Livu win sì txur oe zene (I must be fast and strong)
Ha n(i)'aw (So only)
Pxan livu txo nì'aw oe ngari (Only if I am worthy of you)
Tsakrr nga Na'viru yomtìyìng (Will you feed the People).

X-BOW

The x-bow is used for hunting and for protection from animals.

The X shape of the bow makes it very powerful. With that extra power, the bow can be used to hunt large animals like hammerhead titanotheres or banshees.

The x-bow is six feet long and weighs eleven pounds. It is made from wood and is decorated with twine and paint. Na'vi use the x-bow to hunt from their banshees in the air but not from direhorses on the ground. The x-bow is so long it could get caught on trees if Na'vi hunters used it in the forest.

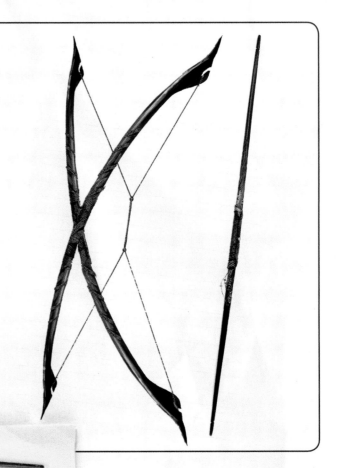

WARBONNETS

The warbonnet is a beautiful plant that has shimmering leaves. The leaves are bioluminescent. During some special dances, the Na'vi wear a huge warbonnet on their heads.

The Na'vi also use the leaves of the warbonnet to mark paths, sort of like the lights you might have along a walk leading up to your front door.

HAMMERHEAD TITANOTHERE

The hammerhead looks like a rhino dressed up for a party. But in spite of its fancy appearance, it's a pretty grumpy animal.

The hammerhead uses its "hammer," the big protrusion on its head, to splinter large trees. When the hammerhead is young, the hammer is made of bendable cartilage, just like your ear. That's so the hammerhead doesn't get stuck between trees when it walks through the forest. As it grows up, the hammer part of its head becomes hard bone.

The hammer helps in battles with other big animals like a thanator or the giant leonopteryx.

Hammerheads move in small groups on Pandora's plains. They graze on grass, shrubs, and forest fruit.

Hammerheads have colorful skin flaps on the sides of their heads that they can fan out to make them look even bigger than they are. When fanned out, the flaps can be read as a threat to other animals.

The first humans to see the Hallelujah Mountains thought that they were dreaming. Imagine seeing whole mountains hovering above the ground. When scientists tried to tell other people what they had seen, no one believed them.

But the Hallelujah Mountain range is very real. Some of its "mountains" are as small as boulders and others as big as a city. They move as they float, and sometimes they will crash together. This makes a sound that can be heard for miles. The Na'vi name for the mountains means "thundering rocks."

Why do the Hallelujah Mountains float? If you've ever played with magnets, you've probably noticed that if you turn them a certain way, they pull toward each other. But if you turn them a different way, they push away from, or *repel*, each other. A similar kind of "magnetic field" explains why the Hallelujah Mountains float. There's lots of unobtanium in the mountains and in the ground beneath them. The unobtanium creates a magnetic force that actually pushes the mountains away from the ground, but the weight of the mountains keeps them near the surface—hovering.

The Hallelujah Mountains are very special to the Na'vi. It is here that the flying creatures known as banshees live. It is here that young Na'vi go to select a banshee they will ride and hunt with for the rest of their lives. This is a very special moment for a Na'vi—and a very dangerous one.